Happy Birthday, Tree!
A Tu B'Shevat Story

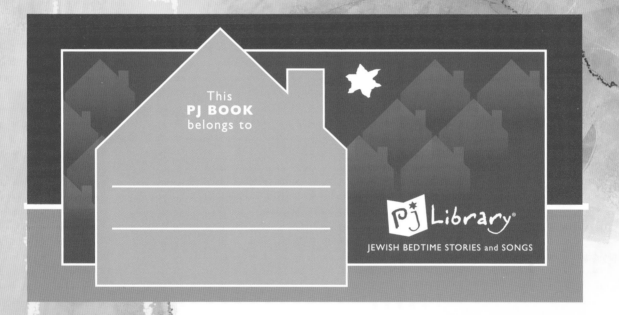

This **PJ BOOK** belongs to

_____

_____

PJ Library®
JEWISH BEDTIME STORIES and SONGS

Madelyn Rosenberg

Illustrated by Jana Christy

Albert Whitman & Company, Chicago, Illinois

For Graham and Karina: Grow and bloom.—M.R.
For Johnny, my tree-planting partner.—J.C.

Library of Congress Cataloging-in-Publication Data

Rosenberg, Madelyn, 1966–
Happy birthday, Tree! : a Tu B'Shevat story / by Madelyn Rosenberg ;
illustrated by Jana Christy.
p. cm.
Summary: Joni and Nate figure out how to celebrate a tree's birthday for Tu B'Shevat.
ISBN 978-0-8075-3151-8 (hardcover)
[1. Tu B'Shevat—Fiction. 2. Trees—Fiction. 3. Jews—Fiction.] I. Christy, Jana, ill. II. Title.
PZ7.R71897Hap 2012 [E]—dc23 2011034187

The design is by Carol Gildar.

For more information about Albert Whitman & Company,
please visit our web site at www.albertwhitman.com

011421.5K2

Note

Tu B'Shevat is a Jewish holiday known as "the New Year for Trees" or "the Birthday of the Trees." It's celebrated on the fifteenth of the Jewish month of Shevat—January or February on our calendar. That's the time of year that trees first begin to bloom in Israel, although it's winter in North America. Long ago, in ancient Israel, this was the day to determine how much of a crop would be used to help support Jewish priests, a practice called *tithing*. These days, Tu B'Shevat is more like Arbor Day, a celebration of trees and a reminder to take care of our environment and our earth. In Israel, families often plant trees on Tu B'Shevat. In other countries, people often send money to plant trees in Israel, or they might plant trees themselves in warmer climates. Another way of celebrating is with a Tu B'Shevat seder, where participants eat from Israel's seven species mentioned in the Torah: barley, dates, figs, grapes, olives, pomegranates, and wheat.

Joni climbed the tree that grew tall and quiet in her front yard. Today was Tu B'Shevat, the Birthday of the Trees. But Joni's tree didn't look like it was celebrating. It didn't look like it even knew it was having a birthday.

"Happy Birthday, Tree!" Joni yelled so her voice would reach the highest branch. She sang the birthday song in Hebrew and English. The tree just stood there.

"I know what you need," Joni said. "A party!" She climbed down
and ran next door to Nate's house.

"Today is the Birthday of the Trees," she announced.
"And we're having a party."
  "What do you get a tree for its birthday?" Nate asked.
Joni thought a minute. "Water?" she suggested.

"Water is boring," Nate said.

"But trees need it," said Joni. So they filled the watering can
and poured water on the tree. The tree looked a little happier.

"What else?" asked Joni.

"Sunshine," Nate said. "Sunshine isn't boring."

They looked up. Clouds covered the sun.

"Blow," Joni said. Joni and Nate blew and blew until the sun peeked out.

The tree looked even happier.

"Now what?" Nate said.

"Cupcakes!"

Joni loved cupcakes. Together she and Nate made a giant one out of the cool soil. The tree didn't take a single bite, but Joni and Nate thought it looked happier.

"A good tree needs a good bird," Joni said. She ran to the house
and came back with Daisy, her souvenir swan from the botanical garden.

"Swans don't live in trees," Nate said, but Joni stuck Daisy in the
bend of a branch anyway.

The tree was still.

"Maybe it just wants to be with other trees," Nate said.

Joni and Nate reached their arms high into the air to make branches. When the wind came, they wiggled their fingers like leaves. But after three minutes, their branches felt heavy. After five minutes, their branches really started to ache. And Joni didn't think her mother or Nate's mother would let them stand in the yard after dark.

"I have an idea," Joni said. "I know just what our tree needs!" She ran to the house to tell her mother. Then she found her piggy bank and her mother's purse and car keys.

At the nursery, Joni's mother followed Joni and Nate among rows and rows of trees.

"Look!" Joni said. "The bottoms are all wrapped up—like presents!"

"Those are the roots," her mother said. "The burlap keeps the soil packed around them so they can stay safe and moist until the tree is planted."

At first it was hard to choose. Then Joni saw a little tree that reminded her of the big tree back home. Someday it would make a good climbing tree, she thought. But it was already the right size to be just what her big tree needed: a friend.

"This one!" Joni said.

When Joni's father came home, Joni, her mother, and Nate were digging a hole for the little tree across the yard from the big one.

They placed the tree in the hole and gently removed the burlap. When they were sure the tree was comfortable, they patted the dirt back into place.

Then they gave the little tree a drink of water and some mulch . . .

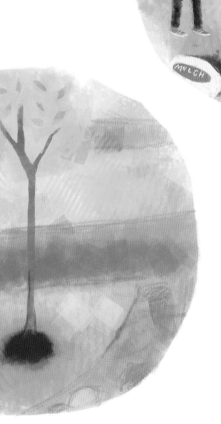

and welcomed it with a prayer.

Joni brushed off her hands and stood in the shadow of the big tree.
"Happy birthday, Tree!" she said again. "Now we can have our party."
She passed out the newspaper hats she'd made for her own birthday.
She gave a hat to each tree, and to Nate, and to her parents, and to
some of the neighbors who had gathered around to watch.

"Wait," Nate said. "Shouldn't we give something to the new tree? And what about my trees? It's their birthday, too."

Nate had a yard full of trees. There weren't enough party hats for them. Or for the Huffmans' trees or the Kims' trees or the Baxters'.

Joni chewed on her lip and thought about what she could give the little tree—and all of the big ones. She spun around in a circle. She hopped on one foot.

Then she decided. A promise.

"I will take care of you, Little Tree," Joni said. "I promise to protect you and water you and love you. I promise I'll be good to you, Tree. I'll be good to the trees of the world."

Her mother smiled. Her father winked.
"We promise, too!" everyone shouted.

The trees looked happy. They waved their branches
and rattled their leaves. Joni stood on the ground
between them. When she closed her eyes it sounded—
just a bit—as if the trees were clapping.